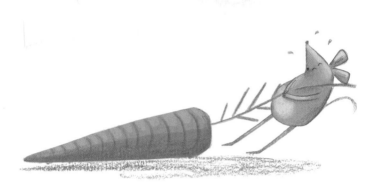

This book belongs to

. . . .

For my brother, Daniel.

OXFORD
UNIVERSITY PRESS

Great Clarendon Street, Oxford OX2 6DP
Oxford University Press is a department of the University of Oxford.
It furthers the University's objective of excellence in research, scholarship,
and education by publishing worldwide in

Oxford   New York

Auckland Cape Town Dar es Salaam Hong Kong Karachi
Kuala Lumpur Madrid Melbourne Mexico City Nairobi
New Delhi Shanghai Taipei Toronto

With offices in

Argentina Austria Brazil Chile Czech Republic France Greece
Guatemala Hungary Italy Japan Poland Portugal Singapore
South Korea Switzerland Thailand Turkey Ukraine Vietnam

Oxford is a registered trade mark of Oxford University Press
in the UK and in certain other countries

British Library Cataloguing in Publication Data
Data available

ISBN: 978-0-19-275680-0 (paperback)
1 3 5 7 9 10 8 6 4 2

Printed in China

Paper used in the production of this book is a natural,
recyclable product made from wood grown in sustainable forests.
The manufacturing process conforms to the environmental
regulations of the country of origin.

CHICKENS CAN'T SEE IN THE DARK

KRISTÝNA LITTEN

OXFORD
UNIVERSITY PRESS

On Sunnyside Farm, there is one chicken
that all the other chickens are talking about.

SUNNYSIDE FARM

And her name is Little Pippa.

It all started when Mr Benedict told his class,
'As sure as eggs is eggs, chickens can't see in the dark.'

Little Pippa was very disappointed.
She wanted to see in the dark more than anything.

And she knew someone
who might be able to help.

As soon as school was over,
she went to Mr Owl's tree house.

'A chicken who wants to see in the dark?' said Mr Owl. 'What a hoot!' And he laughed so much he nearly fell off his chair.

'Mr Owl wasn't very helpful at all,' thought Little Pippa.

So she decided to go to Miss Featherbrain's library instead.

Miss Featherbrain looked puzzled when Pippa asked where she could find a book about seeing in the dark.

'Chickens can't see in the dark!' she said. 'That's just an old hens' tale.'

So Pippa searched HIGH and LOW

until she found a book called

OLD HENS' TALES.

And there it was!

TALE NUMBER 264:

CARROTS
HELP
YOU
SEE
IN
THE
DARK.

SHHH!

TALE·264

'CARROTS!

I need carrots!'
Pippa squawked.
And off she scrambled . . .

to the farm shop.

'What's a little chicken like you
going to do with all those carrots?'
asked Granny Bumblefoot.

'I'm going to see in the dark,'
said Little Pippa.

'Oh my feet and feathers!'
laughed Granny Bumblefoot.

'Chickens seeing in the dark? Whatever next!'

But Pippa was already on her way home.

She wanted to find out how many carrots would help her see in the dark.

She ate one carrot.

Then two.

Then three.

After carrot number four,
Pippa decided the best thing to do
would be to eat **all** the carrots . . .

so she hurried to
Mother Hen's Pantry
to cook up the biggest
carrot banquet ever.

Little Pippa made . . .

MOTHER HEN'S
Pantry

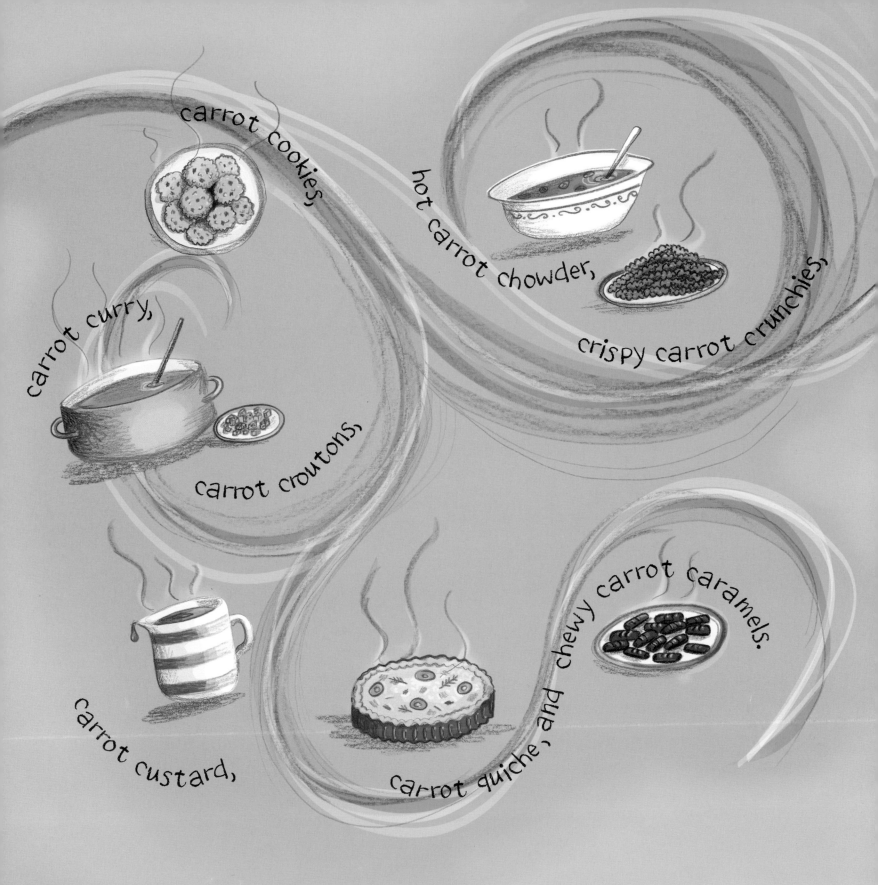

carrot cookies,

hot carrot chowder,

crispy carrot crunchies,

carrot curry,

carrot croutons,

carrot custard,

carrot quiche, and chewy carrot caramels.

The delicious smells of Little Pippa's banquet wafted over Sunnyside Farm.

And before you could say cock-a-doodle-doo, all the chickens were outside Mother Hen's Pantry.

MOTHER HEN'S
Pantry

'I'm going to be the first chicken that can see in the dark!' said Pippa, as she got ready to spread out her carrot feast.

The chickens looked at each other and laughed.

Then they looked at the cookies, quiches, custards, curries, cordials, and cupcakes.

It all looked very tasty.
It looked impossible to resist.

As the sky grew dark . . .

the chickens gasped with delight. They could see
things they had never seen before: twinkly stars,
shimmery shadows, and the beautiful moon.

'We were wrong
and you were right!'
they squawked as they
gathered around Pippa.

'Chickens **can** see in the dark!'

Mr Benedict gave Pippa a friendly pat
and Miss Featherbrain gave her a peck on the cheek,
which made Pippa blush.

Or perhaps it was just all those carrots!